BERYL
THE RAINMAKER

BERYL
THE RAINMAKER

by
JOAN PHIPSON
Illustrated by Laszlo Acs

HAMISH HAMILTON
LONDON

First published in Great Britain 1984 by
Hamish Hamilton Children's Books
27 Wrights Lane, London W8 5TZ
Copyright © 1984 by Joan Phipson
Illustrations copyright © 1984 by Laszlo Acs

Reprinted 1987

British Library Cataloguing in Publication Data
Phipson, Joan
    Beryl the rainmaker.—(Antelope books)
    I. Title
    823'.914[J]
    ISBN 0-241-11238-9

Filmset in Linotron 202 Baskerville by
Katerprint Co Ltd, Oxford
Printed in Great Britain at the University Press, Cambridge

Chapter One

"YOU'D BETTER WARN Beryl about snakes," said Mrs Morgan on their very first day in the new house.

"Why?" said Mr Morgan. "She's not likely to meet one between this house and her school. It's only two blocks away."

"We're in the country now, remember," said Mrs Morgan.

Mr Morgan sighed. "Beryl," he said to his daughter in a tired voice, "If you see a snake you are not to tread on it, or pick it up, or let it bite you."

"I know," said Beryl. "And I know about poisonous spiders and wasps and stinging nettles."

"You see?" said her father. "She already knows. Even in city schools they teach them things like this."

But there was one thing she didn't know about. When she found it three days later, she had no idea what it was that she had found.

On this first morning she set off for her new school with her six-year-old brother, Teddy, attached to her by one hand and her bag in the other. Her sister, Patty, walked beside the fence, dragging a stick against the palings.

Patty was nine and did not need her hand held.

"Do what Beryl tells you, please," called their mother as she shut the front gate. Mrs Morgan found there was something comforting about the sight of Beryl's short, square back view. Her straight shoulders and those strong, short legs marching forward so purposefully were quite a soothing sight. Even the pigtail of pale, straight hair, hanging like a ramrod down her spine was reassuring. From the front, if she could have seen it, Beryl looked even more calm and confident. Her mouth and fringe made two straight lines across her face and her eyes looked out beneath the fringe very wide and stern and blue.

But inside she was not quite so confident. She was wondering how she would get on with a lot of country children. Would they like her? Would they think she was funny? And would she like them? She was already quite sure she would think they were funny. And she missed the bus and train ride between home and school that she had been used to. It always gave her time to change from Beryl-at-home to Beryl-at-school. When she arrived at this school she didn't know which she would be – just an uncomfortable sort of betwixt and between.

It wasn't as bad as she had expected. The children weren't, after all, very different from the ones she was used to. And she was so busy getting Patty and Teddy into their right places, and comforting Teddy when he found he was going to be in a different building all on his own, that she hardly thought of herself at all until she was in the classroom. Then she found she was so

busy working out what she was expected to know that the others knew and she did not, and what she already knew that they did not, that she stopped worrying about anything else.

In the playground afterwards she listened while they all talked together. "My Dad let me drive the tractor the other day."

"That's nothing. I been using the scoop in the dam. We want to get it cleared out before the rain comes. Dad said he might put me on the payroll, even."

"We got three foxes last night. My big brother, he shot 'em. Beaut skins. Still got winter pelts."

"You going to the pony club Saturdee, Raylene?"

It was a new world to Beryl. She would have to learn about it because she was a friendly person and wanted to make friends and because she liked to help people, and how could she help them if she did not know anything about them?

Beryl's parents had often talked to one another about her helpfulness. "She's such a *good* girl," said Mrs Morgan. "Look at the way she looks after Patty and Teddy."

"Some people might call it bossy," said her father.

"It's a good fault," said Mrs Morgan

quickly, ready to defend her daughter to the last gasp. "And it's her only one."

"Oh no," said Mr Morgan. "She has a worse one."

"And what may that be?" said Mrs Morgan in an ominous voice.

"Sometimes she's jealous," said Mr Morgan. "I've watched her when you take too much notice of the other two."

"Oh, that," said Mrs Morgan, as if he had mentioned a speck on her nose. "That's nothing. It's perfectly natural."

Now, in the school playground, Beryl was looking carefully at the other girls and boys, deciding which of them she would like for a friend. There was a girl called Tracy she thought might do. And Tracy seemed to like her, because she never missed an opportunity of coming to talk to her. Tracy was thin, and freckled and quiet, and she lived on a farm ten kilometres out of town. When

she talked at all, she talked about sheep and cattle and crops, and whether her mother's hens were laying or not. Beryl asked Tracy so many questions that on the second day of their friendship Tracy said, "Come home with me after school tomorrow, eh? I'll show you our farm."

"Oh, yes, please," said Beryl. And then she stopped. "How will I get there?" she asked.

"In the bus," said Tracy, looking surprised. "Same as I do."

"How will I get back?" said Beryl.

"Dad'll drive you back," said Tracy. "He never minds, unless he's busy. He won't be busy."

So on the third day Beryl's mother came to collect Patty, Teddy and her school bag, and she climbed into the bus with Tracy.

It did not take long to get out of the town, and soon the bus was rolling along empty roads between open paddocks where there were sheep and cattle. Here and there were very smooth-looking paddocks that seemed to be spread with green velvet.

"Crops," said Tracy. She sighed, and suddenly looked sad.

"What's the matter?" said Beryl.

"The crops need rain," said Tracy.

Beryl thought it was a strange thing

to be sad about, but she forgot about it quite soon when the bus stopped and Tracy said, "This is where we get out."

Tracy said goodbye to the bus driver and climbed down, and Beryl climbed down after her. The bus door shut and the bus moved off and they were left standing in an empty road between empty paddocks. Beryl looked about her and felt a strange, empty feeling. "Lonely, isn't it?" she said.

Tracy looked quite astonished. "This is home," she said. "Come on."

Beryl saw then that they were

standing by a gate in the fence and a gravel track led from the gate out across the paddock.

"You can't see the house from here," said Tracy. "But it's not far. Mum only picks me up in the car when it's raining." She lifted the chain off the gate and opened it for Beryl. Before she shut it she lifted the lid of the big, round, iron mailbox, pulled out some letters and papers and stuffed them into her school bag. "It's mail day," she said.

They set off down the track, Tracy on

her long, thin, brown legs and Beryl on her short pink, plump ones. There was a small hill on their right, and the track curved round it to the left. When it started to curve Tracy left it and went straight on across the grass towards the hill.

"This is a short cut," she said. "We can cut across the creek in the scrub on the other side."

They climbed up the hill and when they came to the top they could see the country spreading away all round them and not far away a house and some sheds and a little garden.

"That's our house," said Tracy. "Not far, is it?"

Beryl was not used to climbing even little hills and she had to wait until she had stopped puffing before she answered. "How do we get there?" she said. "There are all those trees and

things down there, and all that water."

"Easy," said Tracy. "Follow me." And she began to run down the hill. Beryl ran after her, and her pigtail flapped and swung as she ran. When Tracy reached the edge of the patch of scrub she waited.

Beryl's face was pinker than ever and her eyes were wider and bluer than ever by the time she reached Tracy. But she looked happy and excited. "Do we go in there?" she said as soon as she could speak. And she pointed to the dark shadows in among the bushes and under the trees.

Tracy nodded. "Keep behind me and watch where I go. I know the place to get over the creek." Before Beryl could answer her she had stepped in between two bushes, pushing their branches aside, and had disappeared completely. Only the waving branches told where she had gone in. Beryl plunged after her.

She found that the bushes grew thickest round the edge because they were all pressing out for air and sunlight. Once she got through them she came to a more open part, down near where the water ran. The ground was damp and dark, and overhead the trees spread their branches and the leaves rustled softly in the afternoon breeze. For the moment she could not see Tracy, for her eyes were still dazzled by sunlight. It seemed unnaturally dark where she stood, and a cold chill wrapped round her bare legs. An odd feeling crept through her. It was something she had never felt before. She looked quickly all round her, expecting to see someone – not Tracy – but someone huge and dark and powerful. And she had a feeling he was up among the branches hanging over her. But there was no one there, and presently the feeling slowly went away. As it grew less she recognized it. It was fear. It was not ordinary fear, like expecting to be

hurt, but a fear of finding herself somehow melting away – disappearing and turning into nothing. Beryl never screamed, but she almost called out, and her mouth had started to open when she saw Tracy.

"This way," said Tracy. "Mind the boggy bits."

Everything became ordinary again and it was not so cold after all. Beryl decided she had been breathing too hard. The oxygen, or whatever it was, must have done something funny to her brain. She was quite recovered now, and she thought no more about it.

"Coming," she shouted. "I couldn't see you for a minute." And she marched forward in Tracy's footsteps.

It was not a very big creek, but the soak from the hill had made a wide boggy patch under the trees. There were hard bits and a few stones here and there that made it easy to cross when you knew where to step. On the far side, right in the middle of the patch of scrub grew a big eucalyptus tree. Its wide trunk reared up, shining and ghostly in the gloom. Its branches spread out above like protecting arms and its roots clutched, muscular and nobbly, at the land it grew out of. Some of them even grew out into the water, and Beryl could see bunches of little red threads coming from them – baby roots, reaching into the flowing stream.

Tracy waited until Beryl was safely across the water and then began to push her way through the bushes on the other side. She did not notice that Beryl had bent down and was busy scraping the mud off her shoe. So she did not see her stop, look towards the big tree and then pick something out from among its twisted roots.

Beryl had seen the sparkling thing
deep among the roots of the tree as she
bent down. When she had scraped the
mud off her shoes she stepped in among

19

the roots, pushing away the dead leaves and strands of grass. She could see the stone tucked in a cavity where two roots crossed. She reached in and picked it up. It was not a very big stone, but it sparkled prettily, even in the shadows. It came up bright and shining when she rubbed it clean on her skirt, and because it was pretty and not too big she put it into her pocket. It was just a piece of stone, and she thought no more about it, but hurried on after Tracy.

Chapter Two

THE HOUSE WHERE Tracy lived was big
and rambling, and verandas all the way
round it made the rooms inside rather
dark. But Beryl thought they were
comfortable sorts of rooms, where a
person could make a mess without its
being very much noticed. The chairs
and tables looked well used, as if they
were quite accustomed to people sitting
about on them, or in them, and were
prepared to make everybody as comfortable as they could. Tracy's mother,
Mrs Fielding, was as comfortable and
accommodating as the furniture, and
seemed really pleased that Beryl had
come to see them.

"Tracy tells me you're from the city," she said when Beryl had been brought to her kitchen. "You've never been to the country before?" Beryl shook her head. "Then I expect you'll want to see the dogs and the hens and the wool-shed. And I think they've got some sheep in the yards this afternoon. You take her round and show her, Tracy, and when you come back the scones will be out of the oven."

It was in the sheep yards that they met Mr Fielding. He was a tall, thin man with a kind face that Beryl thought looked rather worried. The lines across his forehead and on each side of his mouth suggested that perhaps he worried quite a lot. Beryl was sorry because he smiled at her so nicely and she wondered, as she always did when she thought people were in trouble, what she could do to help him. But as she

had no idea what he could be worrying about, and everything looked so peaceful in the afternoon spring sunshine, she could only smile back and wait to be told what the troubles were.

There was a lot of noise and quite a bit of dust everywhere. Sheep were bleating and running round in the yards and some were hurrying along a narrow laneway between the yards, and a man on the far side was sticking something into their mouths as they passed. Dogs were barking and the dust rose up in clouds.

"Sorry it's so dusty," said Tracy's father. "Shouldn't be, this time of year. But we're needing rain. Ever seen sheep being drenched before?"

"Drenched?" said Beryl, for they looked quite dry to her.

"Medicine," said Tracy. "For worms."

Perhaps that was why Tracy's father looked so worried – because his sheep were sick. "Are they ill, then?" said Beryl.

"Not really ill," said Mr Fielding, and gave her his pleasant smile. "Sheep

25

often have worms, and now and then we have to do something about it." It didn't sound the sort of thing he was worrying about. The sheep went on running through the race and the dogs drove them through a yard and out into the paddocks, where they began to graze about quite happily.

After that, Tracy took her to see the woolshed and the fowlyards, and they collected the eggs and shut the hens up for the night. "So the foxes don't get them," said Tracy. They looked at the garden, where the blossom was beginning to come out.

"I'd grow vegetables if it was me," said Beryl as they went in to Mrs Fielding and the scones.

It wasn't until Mr Fielding and Tracy were driving Beryl home again that she found out what was worrying him. They passed the paddocks where

the crop was, and Mr Fielding said,
"It's not looking as good as it did."

It still looked like green velvet to
Beryl, and in the fading daylight it was
hard to see anything specially wrong

with it. But Mr Fielding said, "It's not growing the way it did."

"Why not?" said Beryl, who felt quite at home with Mr Fielding now.

Her question seemed to surprise him. He looked away from the road ahead for a moment, to observe her round, shining face beside him. "Rain," he said. "We need rain. We need it now, badly."

"Oh," said Beryl, and knew at last what was worrying him.

So when they reached her house and she was thanking him and saying good-bye, she looked up into his face and said very earnestly, "I do hope it rains for you, Mr Fielding. I'll *will* it to rain for you." And she said it with such fervour that she clenched her hands as she spoke, and without her realizing it her left hand curled round the stone in her pocket, which she had already forgotten. Her hot palm pressed against it.

"So do I," said Mr Fielding, "and if your willing it will make it rain, please go on doing so. We'll be very grateful."

Chapter Three

THAT NIGHT A great explosion of sound woke Beryl from a sleep that was fathoms deep. It was so deep that it took her a minute to think where she was. Her nerves still twitched with fright, and the noise still seemed to be rolling round her bedroom by the time she was wide awake. Then came a great flash of light through the window, and suddenly the bedroom was as bright as day. She just had time to notice that everything was still where she expected it to be when the light went out. There came another great boom, and at last she knew it was thunder that had woken her. She clambered out of bed and shut the window, because the curtain had started to blow out over her bed like a great flag. She had only just

got back when the rain came. It battered the iron roof, blotting out every other sound. And soon she could hear it rattling down the gutters and splashing into the old iron tank that still stood behind the house. It was quite a big storm, and for some time the flashes of lightning lit up the room, and the sound of thunder came over the roaring of the rain on the roof.

Beryl sighed happily, thinking of Mr Fielding and his crop. She slid down into her warm bed, pulled the blankets up round her ears and listened to the lovely water tumbling on to the earth.

Next day Tracy ran up to her as soon as she arrived. Her face was bright with smiles. "Isn't it lovely? Just what Dad wanted. He said if it had been any harder it would have washed the crop clean away. He says he'll let you know when he wants it to rain again." She burst into laughter and slid her arm through Beryl's. "Isn't he funny?"

Beryl was much too sensible to think the rain really had anything to do with her, but all the same, it was nice to pretend she had brought it for him.

It was several weeks before she went to Tracy's house again. In the meantime Tracy had come to hers, and Mrs Morgan had driven her home afterwards, exclaiming at the loneliness of it. Winter was sliding away into the back of people's minds and the days were getting longer and hotter. The land was getting drier, too, for the winter's clouds rolled away, leaving clear skies and floods of sunshine. So that when she saw Mr Fielding again he was again wearing his worried look, though this time it was not quite so agonized.

"The crops need rain," said Beryl, peering into his face.

"I can't deny it," said Mr Fielding. "We could do with a drop more now."

"I'll do my best," said Beryl, and they all laughed. She looked up into the clear blue sky, clenched her hands tightly again and said loudly, "I *will* it to rain again for Mr Fielding – but not quite so hard as last time," she added. And because she was wearing the same jacket as last time, and because she had forgotten all about the stone in her pocket and it was still there, her hand closed on it as it had the time before.

Driving back to town that evening they stopped to let Mr Fielding look closely at his crop. It was long and thick now, and waving like the waves of the sea in the evening wind.

"I could eat it, it's so lovely," said Beryl.

Nothing woke her that night, but when she opened her eyes in the morning the sun was no longer pouring in through the window. There were black clouds instead and it was raining gently.

This time Tracy greeted her without a smile and with eyes that were very wide. It was almost as if she were afraid of Beryl. "You did it again," she said.

Beryl could only nod. There was no smile on her face, either. Somehow, after that they did not speak of rain again.

About a week later Beryl was sitting in the classroom, half listening to the teacher. The air was still and warm in the room and she was half asleep. The words flowed over her, soothing and unremarked. From among them two words suddenly penetrated her half-asleep mind. MAGIC STONES. They were exciting words, and somehow they sent a particular thrill through her

mind. All at once she was wide awake
and listening.

" – probably the Aborigines used
these magic stones for various purposes.
The purpose we mainly know is that of
rain making. Very often the stone is of
quartz crystal and its gleaming surface
irresistably suggests water – "

Beryl's mind flew back to the jacket, now at home in the cupboard, with the stone still in its pocket. She was so busy with this startling idea that she quite forgot to listen to anything further the teacher was saying. This was a pity, because the teacher explained that there were also magics for stopping rain, as well as for making it. She could hardly wait for the end of the day to get back home and feel in the pocket of her jacket.

Tracy was not in the same class as Beryl, so Beryl waited after school to catch her and tell her all about it. But as she waited she began to think. It was something she could hardly believe herself, though she did believe it in a strange way. She remembered now, how her hand had closed on that hard, cold, angular piece of stone as she wished so hard for the rain. But perhaps Tracy would find it all too hard to believe. Like Beryl, Tracy was a practical girl and believed in things that she could touch and see. It was only that Beryl had had this funny experience and she had not. Beryl decided she would not tell Tracy just yet. She would wait and experiment with the stone and see what happened. The secret was so big inside her that when Tracy found her she asked kindly if she was feeling well, for she looked as if she had a pain in her middle.

For the rest of that day and all the waking hours of that night the strangest sensations kept passing through her. It is a very powerful feeling indeed to find you can, all of a sudden, control the weather. But it is a frightening feeling, too. She was not yet quite sure that this was what she was really able to do, but as soon as she saw that Patty and

Teddy were well out of the way she
slipped into her bedroom, shut the door
and went to the cupboard. The jacket
was still there where she had hung it.
She was a neat and tidy person. She
took it out, carried it to the bed and felt

in the pocket. The first bump of her fingertips on the cold stone sent a quiver through her. Holding her breath, she felt for it, let it slip into her hand and pulled it out. Then she took it to the window and opened her hand. It lay there, the small, angular piece of crystal, gleaming and sparkling in the late sunlight on the window sill. Should she try it now, this very minute? The excitement was terrific and she almost forgot to breathe as she closed her hand on it again. She was just about to say the words she had used before when she saw Patty and Teddy run across the lawn beside the house. Teddy was holding the string of a kite and Patty was shouting to him to run faster. The kite had caught the wind and was high over their heads, almost as high as the big tree by the gate. It was frail, and big and beautiful, like an enormous but-

terfly. In fact, it was shaped like a butterfly. But it was only made of paper. It was flying so well, and they were so clever to have got it into the air. She opened her hand again, and the air went out of her lungs in a sound that was almost like a wail. A few drops of rain would ruin the kite forever and she could not risk it.

The secret continued to burn inside her for several days. Patty and Teddy complained that she was cross. Her mother kept feeling her forehead for signs of a temperature. Her father told her, but not too unkindly, to pull herself together.

Chapter Four

MRS MORGAN was learning to fit into her new country life, and one of the new things she was doing was to plant vegetables. Like Beryl, she preferred to do things that had a positive result. Beryl often helped her. They were looking at the young beans together one day. They had watched, fascinated, from the time the first whitey-green, bent-over little leaves had pushed their way unbelievably out of the ground. They had watched while they straightened themselves out, reached for the sky, became a darker green and began to grow tall. But today Mrs Morgan said, "I don't think they look so well today. It's all this dry weather."

In a kind of whisper Beryl said, "Do you think they need some rain?"

"Oh, I think so," said Mrs Morgan. "In fact, I think all the garden could do with a drop of rain now. It must be weeks since we had the last lot. Watering is never the same."

When they returned to the house Beryl went thoughtfully to her room. The stone was still in the jacket pocket, where she had decided it was safest. She took it out and looked at it. It seemed as bright as ever. Then she went to the door and locked it. She stood in the middle of the room, screwed up her eyes, squeezed her hand tight on the piece of quartz and said, "I want it to rain. It *will* rain. It *will* rain. I *will* it to rain."

It took her a long time to go to sleep that night. As far as she could see, the

weather was unchanged. For a long
time she watched the stars in their slow
procession across her windowpane.
Then, at last, she went to sleep. It was

an uneasy sleep, full of dark dreams that were not quite nightmares, but almost. After one dream more distressing than the others, where the invisible presence she had felt under the trees by the creek seemed to be pressing down on her, she woke with a gasp. She found herself sitting bolt upright in bed, clutching the blanket which had left her feet and had come slithering up round her throat. She pushed it back and was prepared to slide down again when she realized that the soft hissing noise that she had thought part of the dream was still going on. For a few minutes she sat up straight and stiff, breathing as softly as she could and listening. Then she crept out of bed and went to the window. It was open and she looked out. It was raining. It was a soft and gentle rain, but it was very steady, and when she looked up she could not see a star anywhere.

Mrs Morgan was very happy next morning. It was still raining gently, and she looked out of the window and said, "My beans will grow like mad now. We'll be eating them before long, I wouldn't be surprised."

Beryl had come in to breakfast not knowing whether to be pleased and proud, or rather frightened. It was a very big power to find oneself with at ten years old. But seeing her mother so happy, and knowing now that it was what she had been able to do that had made her happy, took all the fright out of her. She felt instead a great swelling of pride and strength. She thought of all the good things she would be able to do for people and her round, pink face shone beneath its curtain of fringe.

"I believe Beryl's as happy about the beans as you are," Mr Morgan said to her mother.

"It's not – " Beryl started to say, and then stopped. She put a spoonful of cornflakes into her mouth quickly so that she was not able to answer at once when her father said, "Well, tell us, Beryl."

But it was a secret too big to tell. The power that she now had was only hers alone so long as she was the only one who knew. Once they knew about it, her parents would for a certainty start telling her how to use it, and Patty and Teddy, who were already looking at her curiously, would tell everyone within hearing as soon as they got to school. As well as being a kind girl, Beryl was also a bossy girl, as her father had said. She liked to help people in the way she thought best. So she took a long time to chew the cornflakes, swallowing them as if she feared they would choke her,

49

and then said as casually as she could, "I was only going to say it's not every day you can wish for rain at night and have it by next morning." Even as she said it she wondered if she had said too much. But it had been the only thing that had come into her mind.

Her father was looking puzzled, but her mother said, "Indeed, no. It was a lucky coincidence, wasn't it, Beryl?"

And Beryl hugged her secret tighter than ever.

With so much to think about she had forgotten Tracy and her father's worrying crops. When they met during the morning, Tracy said, "Dad hopes the rain'll take up. We don't need it now."

If Beryl had thought about it at all, she would have assumed that Mr Fielding would have been pleased with the new lot of rain she had brought. She almost began to say she was sorry, but stopped herself just in time. Instead she looked wisely up at the sky and said, "I don't think it'll be much, Tracy. I think it's clearing already," and hoped it was, because the beans were wet enough now.

By lunchtime the sun had come out again and she was now so confident that she began to think she had done it all by herself. For several days after that she did nothing at all about her rain-making stone. Instead, when she was not busy with something else she brooded about it and wondered in what different ways she could make good use of it. She had the strangest feeling she had been given it so that she could help people.

She got a terrible fright one day when she came home from school to find the

jacket laid out on her bed and her mother standing beside it holding the stone in her hand. When Beryl came in she said, "Look what I found in your jacket pocket. Isn't it a pretty stone? I almost sent it to the cleaner by mistake."

Beryl stopped herself just in time from pouncing on it and snatching it out of her mother's hand. Instead she said very quickly and on a strangely high note. "Yes, isn't it? I found it. I thought it would make a nice paperweight." She would never have thought of a paperweight if she had not seen her father's – a globe of glass with a picture inside, and you could make it snow by rolling the globe.

"So it would," said Mrs Morgan. "Here you are, then," and she put it into Beryl's outstretched hand and thought no more about it.

Chapter Five

SPRING FINISHED, summer came, and for
the first week of the Christmas holidays
the Morgan family went to visit Mr
Morgan's father, who had retired to
grow apples in the Blue Mountains.
They found the old man in a fury of
frustration because summer had come
early to the mountains and his young
apple trees were not getting enough
water. "And my new dam hasn't had a
chance to fill up," he said bitterly.

Beryl thought it was very lucky she
had decided it would not be safe to
leave her stone behind, and had
brought it with her secretly, in her
sponge bag. She took it out when

nobody was looking and went away by herself. As she expected, it rained in the night and was still raining next morning. Her grandfather was delighted and kept walking up and down the veranda rubbing his hands.

"Now you're happy, Grandfather, aren't you?" she said kindly.

"I certainly am," he said and walked

to the edge of the veranda. He lifted his head to the wet sky. "Thank you, whoever you are," he shouted happily.

It gave Beryl a pleasantly warm feeling, but she did rather wish he had said it to the right person.

They went home just before Christmas. The rain that had fallen on old Mr Morgan's apple trees had not fallen here. It was quite dry again and the sun shone down on baked earth and wilting plants. Mrs Morgan got busy with the hose and Beryl, watching her, wondered if it would be safe for Mr Fielding's crop if she ordered just a small quantity so that her mother would not have to stand so long in the boiling sun. She would have asked Tracy if Tracy had been there, but she was out on the farm, having her holidays, too. Beryl went into her room and took the stone from her sponge bag. She held it tight,

but not quite as tight as last time, and whispered very quietly, "I will it to rain – just a little."

She was not surprised when clouds rolled up after lunch and her Mother said, "I don't believe I'll have to go out and water this afternoon. I think I'm going to get it done for me."

And sure enough, by four o'clock the rain was falling on the beans and damping down the dust in the garden. Next day she went to the telephone and rang up Tracy. After they had talked about Beryl's holiday, and Christmas, and what a long time it was since they had seen one another, Beryl said, "How is your father's crop?"

Tracy's voice came faintly over the telephone. "Nearly ready for harvesting. It looks great. Got a fright yesterday, though. We got an unexpected shower and Dad wondered if he was going to have it flattened after all. He nearly rang you up to have it stopped." Beryl heard her giggle as she said it.

By the end of the year Mrs Morgan had come to know quite a lot of people in the town. She came home one afternoon looking quite excited and said one of her new friends had asked if she would like to bring all her children to the pony club camp that was to be held the following week. Patty shrieked with delight and began to jump up and down. Teddy looked pleased, but a little doubtful, because he was not sure

he would like having even a small horse too close to him.

Beryl said, "How can we? We haven't any ponies."

"It doesn't matter," said her mother. "We've only been asked to go and watch. We won't have to camp there like the others. We can go each day. And perhaps if you think it would be fun we might persuade Dad to find a pony somewhere next year."

"I'd rather have a motorbike," Teddy said very quickly. But Patty shouted, "I want one. I want one," and tugged at her mother's sleeve.

Beryl said nothing, but she thought of Tracy, and how she and Tracy could ride about together on the farm, for Tracy had learned to ride at about the same time that she had learned to walk. Her smile reached from one side of her face to the other.

Chapter Six

IT WAS JUST before the pony club camp
that the great disaster happened. It was
something that Beryl never afterwards
forgot. Though she did not realize it,
she became a different Beryl afterwards
– a better Beryl, even, though she did
not know it at the time.

She had not used the stone since that
one time when they came back from her
grandfather's house. What Tracy said
had made her think, and she was more
careful now. Everything seemed to be
growing nicely, people were getting
their washing dry without any trouble
and the arrangements for the camp
were going ahead happily under a

benign sky. Then on the afternoon
before they were to go out to the camp,
when all the members were already
riding out to the woolshed where they
were to sleep, Beryl walked into her
bedroom to fetch a book. Ever since her
mother had found the stone she had
kept it, pretending it was, indeed, a
paperweight, on the table beside her
bed, resting on the letters her friends in

the city had written to her. When she decided to leave it there it had seemed to her a very cunning thing to do. She now saw that Teddy was standing in front of the table. His head was bent and he was peering at something he held in his hand. She walked quietly up behind him and looked over his shoulder. It was the stone.

"Give me that," she shouted in his ear, and tried to snatch it from him. He gave a yelp, ducked, and rushed out of the room before she could stop him. And she had seen his hand close round her stone as he yelped. She ran after him, shouting. But she lost him between the bedroom and the back door. She ran outside into the garden, but he was nowhere to be seen. She ran back into the house, into one room after another. She was in a frenzy of anger and acute apprehension. The thought of that power in his small hand, at the mercy of his unbridled whims and fancies made her cold inside. She ran out again, just in time to see him meet Patty, who was coming in at the gate, snatch her hand and pull her off into the bushes. She stopped dead, clenched her teeth and went on silent feet across the lawn and into the other side of the small shrubbery.

By the time she saw them they were climbing up the tree near the gate. She pushed through the bushes, ran to the tree, and managed to grab Teddy's ankle before he could pull his foot out of reach. He tugged, but she held on with both hands, and when he stopped tugging, she tugged. He gave a small cry and she saw his hand come away from the branch it was grasping.

"Let him go," screamed Patty from higher up the tree. "Let him go, Beryl.

He'll fall down."

She held on, and as she looked up at him she saw him make another effort to grab the branch with his free hand. It was the hand that held the stone.

65

Without a thought he hurled it from him and grabbed the branch. The stone flew through the air, glinted for a moment in the sun and then plunged into the bushes below.

Beryl did not usually make uncontrolled or unexpected noises, but now a kind of howl came from her throat and in her rage she put both hands round Teddy's ankle, put her foot against the tree and pulled. There was a crack as the branch broke, a gasp, and Teddy and his branch came down the tree and landed with a thump on the ground. Beryl only just had time to get out of the way. "You killed him," Patty screamed from above.

It certainly looked like it, because he was lying there without moving. Only an appalled look on his face and two staring eyes suggested he was not yet quite dead.

It all happened at the time Mr Morgan came home from work. He was coming through the gate when he heard the noise and caught a glimpse of Patty's jeans half way up the tree. He pushed through the bushes just in time to see his son lying, making strange strangled noises at the foot of the tree.

"Stand back," he said to Beryl, and bent over his son. Nobody moved. Patty, her eyes wide, gazed down through the branches. Presently Mr Morgan stood up. "I think he's only winded. Get your mother, Beryl. Quickly."

By the time Beryl returned, pulling a white-faced Mrs Morgan by the hand, Teddy was sitting up, breathing deeply in a wheezing kind of way. Patty had come down from the tree and was on her knees gazing into his face, horrified, but fascinated. Mr Morgan was rub-

bing his back.

"It's all right," he said, as Mrs
Morgan rushed to pick up her son.

"Leave him alone for a minute. He's only winded, but I want to ask him if anything hurts before we move him."

It was all Mrs Morgan could do not to snatch him up. While she waited she turned to Beryl. "Whatever happened!" she said. Beryl always knew. This time it was Patty who told her.

"Beryl chased him up the tree. He only wanted to look at her old stone." She stopped and for a minute looked closely at Beryl. For once Beryl seemed quite unable to say anything. "Beryl's gone mad, I think," said Patty at last.

There seemed, after all, to be nothing wrong with Teddy once he had got his breath back, but he allowed himself to be carried, sobbing gently and enjoyably, into the house and laid on the sitting-room couch. After a glass of milk and a large slice of cake he felt himself able to rise and announce that he would now go outside and play, and he would like Patty to go with him.

When they had gone, Mr Morgan said, "Beryl," and waited until she had come forward to stand in front of him. Beryl never wilted. She was the wrong shape, but it did seem now as if some of the stiffness had gone out of her. Telling what had happened was not easy, because she could not really explain the terrible thing that Teddy had done. She could only say that she was cross with him for stealing her paperweight.

"But you *pulled* him out of the *tree*," said her mother. "You might have killed him."

There was nothing she could say that would make it sound any better. In the end she was told that she could not possibly go to the pony club camp. How could they risk taking someone capable of such unbridled violence among all the other children? She would stay at home and read her book and her father would be back every lunchtime to see she remained there. The lady next door, whom Mrs Morgan had come to know, would keep an eye on her. Also, there would be no pony for her next year.

She knew she had done an awful thing, but she knew that it was not as awful, knowing all she knew, as they thought. She was on the verge of explaining about the stone just to wipe the look of puzzled sorrow off their faces. But it was a secret she could not bring herself to tell. And even if she did, she thought they would probably not believe her.

So next morning, with fury and misery only just controlled, she watch- ed them go. It was another clear, fine day with blue sky and a warm sun – just the weather for a pony club camp.

When they were out of sight she slipped
out into the garden, being careful the
next-door neighbour could not see her.
She pushed her way into the shrubbery,
not very hopeful that she would ever

find the stone again, but determined to try till she dropped.

For nearly two hours she hunted. She had almost given up hope when she saw it. From a pile of dead leaves came a sudden dazzling flash as a shaft of sunlight caught the crystal. She pounced, shuffling the dead leaves with trembling hands. As she felt it and scooped it up, she sighed a long, long sigh. She stood up, holding it carefully as if it were a holy relic, which, in fact, it was, and carried it back to the house. She went boldly in at the front door. She did not care who saw her.

She went into her room and sat down on the bed. For a few minutes she just sat and gazed at the stone. Then she closed it in her hands, raised her head and began to think of the pony club. She thought of Patty and Teddy and imagined how they would be enjoying themselves. She wondered how they would explain why she wasn't with them. The more she thought, and imagined how happy they were, the more cross she became, and the more jealous that they, who had done nothing to deserve it, should be there. And she who tried so hard to do the best she could for everybody, should have to stay behind. It was not hard to work herself into a state of black jealousy and a feeling that great injustice had been done to her.

"It's not *fair*," her mind screamed. "It's not FAIR!"

And almost, but not quite, without thinking, she held the stone tight and said to herself. "I hope it rains." Having said it once it was easy to say it again. In the end she was standing up holding the stone hard against her chest and whispering in a kind of savage hiss,

"I *will* it to rain. I *will* it to rain. It must go on raining and raining and raining."

Suddenly the violent feelings left her. She walked to the table and put the stone down. Then she went over to the window. She hadn't really wanted to spoil their day, and the day of all the others. What could have got into her? Perhaps it was just a fluke that it had rained those other times. It was all silly, anyway. It was only what the Aboriginals believed. The teacher has said so. It couldn't be true she had been given by a lucky chance so much awful power. She would no longer believe it. She refused to believe it. And she looked at the stone again. It was only a piece of ordinary stone after all. There were lots of bits of quartz about. She had seen them at Tracy's farm.

But by midday the clouds had come up and by three o'clock the rain was

teeming down. At four o'clock Mrs
Morgan and Patty and Teddy came
home, soaking wet.

"They can't do anything," they said. "It's much too wet." People had said this heavy rain couldn't last and it would be all right by tomorrow. But it wasn't. The next day was so wet that it was no use even going out there. And on the third day everyone came home – "washed out", the instructors said.

And now, too late, Beryl remembered Tracy. When she could do so without being overheard she telephoned. "It's awful," said Tracy. "Dad was just about to strip. The crop's going down. If the rain doesn't stop soon there'll be nothing left to strip. Thousands of dollars Dad says we'll lose." There was a pause and then Tracy said, "Dad says you were so good at starting it raining, what about stopping it now? Dad's good. He can always joke – even now."

That night Beryl did not sleep at all. She would have stopped it if she could, but she had not been listening when the teacher had explained about stopping the rain. Nothing she tried was any good. It rained and rained, and soon they were talking about floods.

At last, when Beryl's mother had begun to complain that Beryl was not eating enough and that, surely she must be sickening for something, and when her father had begun secretly to wonder if they had been too hard on her, the rain began to ease. In two days the sun came out and all the land steamed with warmth and new growth. Beryl took her stone, wrapped it in brown paper and put it in the toe of her winter boots.

One day, by chance, she ran into Tracy in the supermarket. The first thing she said was, "How is your Dad's crop?"

Tracy's brown face, bright with delight at seeing her friend, clouded a little. "Dad says we'll save some of it. But a lot's gone. He's stripping now. That's why we're here – to get parts for the stripper." She laughed suddenly and squeezed Beryl's arm. "Dad says you're not nearly as good at stopping it as you are at starting it. But you did in the end, didn't you? I told him you did."

"No," said Beryl soberly. "I couldn't

stop it. I would have stopped it if I could." She was so solemn that Tracy looked at her strangely.

"Well," she said. "Well – I didn't really think – Come on. Let's get a milk shake." And both of them suddenly wanted to forget it all as quickly as they could.

Christmas came and went, the holidays wore on and eventually came to an end. They met at school again and Beryl waited anxiously for Tracy to ask her out to the farm. Tracy went twice to Beryl's house, with Mrs Morgan driving her home afterwards before Beryl found herself at last sitting in the bus beside Tracy. She was looking very preoccupied and the piece of quartz was in her pocket with her hand closed over it. When they came to the patch of scrub Beryl hung back.

"Don't wait," she called. "There's a stone in my shoe. I'll catch up in a minute."

"OK," said Tracy. "It's dry as a bone now. You can cross anywhere." She walked on.

As soon as she was out of sight Beryl stood up. What she had said was almost true. There was a stone, but it was in her pocket. She took it out now, unwrapped it and looked at it. It flashed and sparkled in her hand. It looked pretty and quite harmless, but she knew what its power could be. She knew, too, that it was too big for her. A person had to be strong and wise, and not likely to lose her temper to be able to hold such a power. As she stood looking at it her body began to tingle and the light went out of the small clearing. And for a second time she felt that something she could not see was hovering over her.

She did not know what it meant, but she knew what she had to do. And before Tracy should return to find out what had become of her she walked over the the big tree, bent down and carefully, tenderly, placed the stone in the place where she had found it. She stood up and stepped back, and the clearing grew bright again. All of a sudden she felt well and happy and as if a great load had been shed. She breathed in the clean, eucalyptus-smelling air of the little clearing and shouted, "Tracy, I'm coming. Wait for me." And she ran across the dry bed of the creek, out into the open and the bright summer sunlight.